Two Little Mice
and the
Moon Adventure

by Stuart James

Dedicated to all little adventurers

First published in 2021 by The Happily Ever Press. This story is available in other formats.

ISBN: **979-8-54678-187-3**

TheHappilyEverPress.uk

Ernest, a mouse,
and Elsie, his wife,
lived a happy,
comfortable life
in a hole they had made
in the loft of a pub
with a 'view of the sea,
real ale and good grub.'

Their cupboards were full.
There was much more to plunder.
But Ernest was restless.
He couldn't but wonder ...

He longed for adventure.
He longed for more cheese.
Something unusual ...
A cheese with prestige.

So ...
one starry night,
two little mice
left their mouse hole
to go to sea.
They'd heard in tales
the moon was made
of the finest,
vintage cheese.

They packed in a basket:
nuts, grapes and biscuits
and some other things
they might need,
to set sail for the moon
in half a coconut shell
with an old pillow case
made do for a sail.

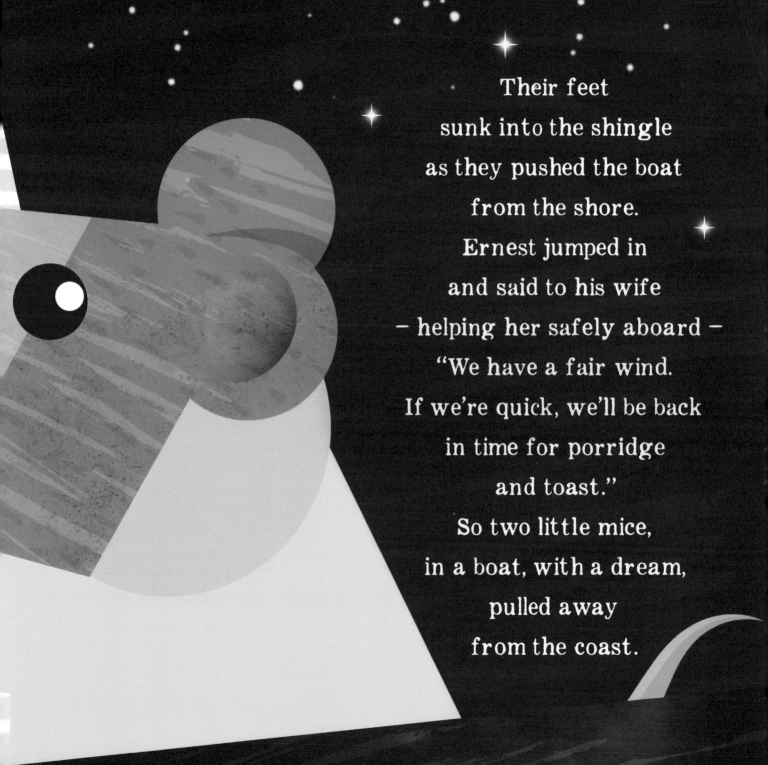

Their feet
sunk into the shingle
as they pushed the boat
from the shore.
Ernest jumped in
and said to his wife
– helping her safely aboard –
"We have a fair wind.
If we're quick, we'll be back
in time for porridge
and toast."
So two little mice,
in a boat, with a dream,
pulled away
from the coast.

The moon had laid
them a path;
a carpet of
shimmering light,
like floating candles
– a million or more –
that flickered
and danced
in the night.

An hour drifted by
but a glance to the sky
told they were no further near.
Yet the home they had left
was barely a speck –
a fading glow

growing dimmer.

Meanwhile the clouds
circled and swelled
and a whistling wind conspired
to rouse the sea
from its deep, calm sleep
and set

a raging
monster
free ...

as tall as a house

sometimes taller

No two mice could ever

have felt smaller ...

as this giant
watery,
tentacled
beast

splashed and thrashed
and spat and teased.

It tossed and rolled them,
spun them round,
nearly turned them

upside down

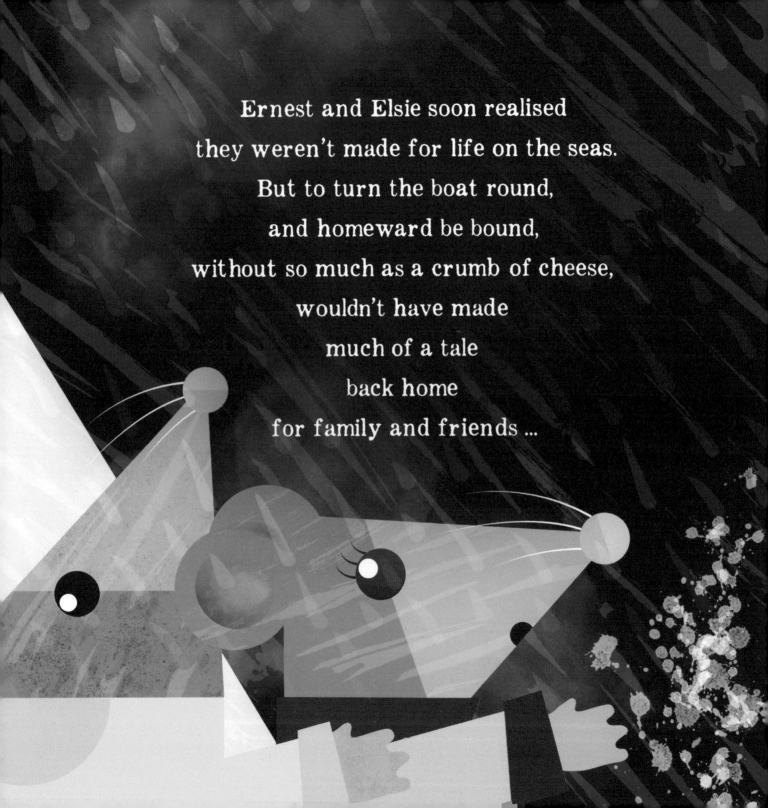

Ernest and Elsie soon realised
they weren't made for life on the seas.
But to turn the boat round,
and homeward be bound,
without so much as a crumb of cheese,
wouldn't have made
much of a tale
back home
for family and friends ...

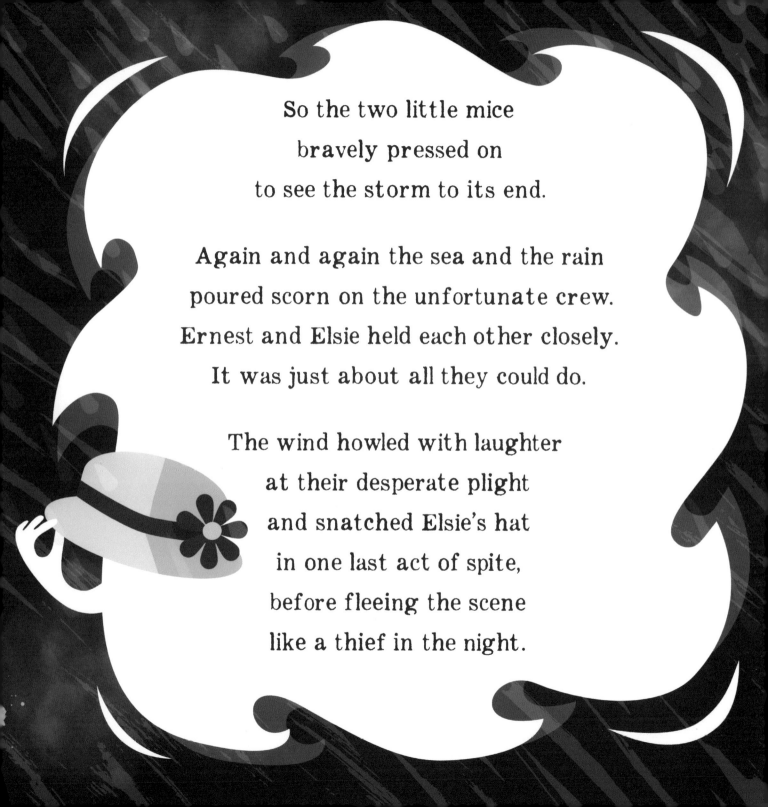

So the two little mice
bravely pressed on
to see the storm to its end.

Again and again the sea and the rain
poured scorn on the unfortunate crew.
Ernest and Elsie held each other closely.
It was just about all they could do.

The wind howled with laughter
at their desperate plight
and snatched Elsie's hat
in one last act of spite,
before fleeing the scene
like a thief in the night.

The clouds, like sheep,
followed behind.
And the sea breathed
a sigh of relief;
the monster within,
laid to rest once again,
a shadowy secret beneath.

Sshhh ...

Then the mice became aware

of a magical light ...

The moon!

so big

and never so bright.

It seemed they could almost

touch it now

– taste it! –

If they could reach somehow.

One by one the stars came on
and made their shapes in the sky.
A crab ... a bear
and over there –
a dolphin leaping high.

A horse ... with wings!
And other things
they could not quite make out.
A swan ... A bell?
A crown as well
and in the corner of the sky –
a jellyfish – no .. spider!
There was no mistaking, why ...

It spun a silken, starry thread
and wove a ladder down,
which hung just above their heads ...
The dream was so close now!
"A little more!"
the mice implored
'til it was at their feet.
"Perfect!" said Ernest,
"Come on, Elsie,
we're in for a treat."

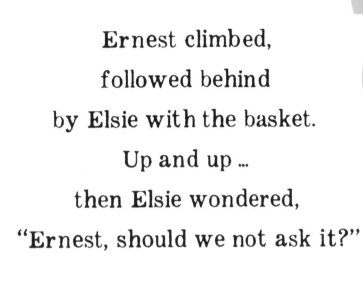

Ernest climbed,
followed behind
by Elsie with the basket.
Up and up ...
then Elsie wondered,
"Ernest, should we not ask it?"

But Ernest now was nearly there,
a cheese-knife in his paw.
He didn't think the moon would miss
a slice or two ... or more.

Then Elsie cried out
desperately
**"Ernest!
Look behind you!"**
Ernest spun around
and was horrified to find who
he really didn't want to see,
now they had come
this far ...

So big. So real. So frightening;
slowly creeping through the stars –
with arched back
and tail held high –
the shape of a cat
with a glint in his eye!

The creature hissed ...
Then pounced ...
But missed
as Ernest scrambled down.
He called to Elsie, down below,

"Turn the boat around!"

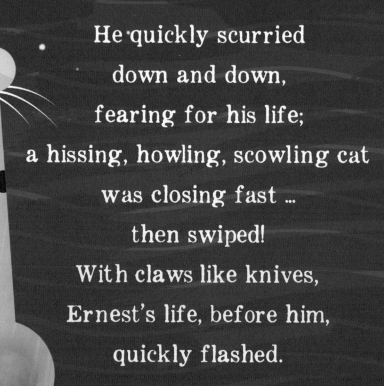

He quickly scurried
down and down,
fearing for his life;
a hissing, howling, scowling cat
was closing fast ...
then swiped!
With claws like knives,
Ernest's life, before him,
quickly flashed.

"Jump!"
cried Elsie

and just in time
Ernest did ...

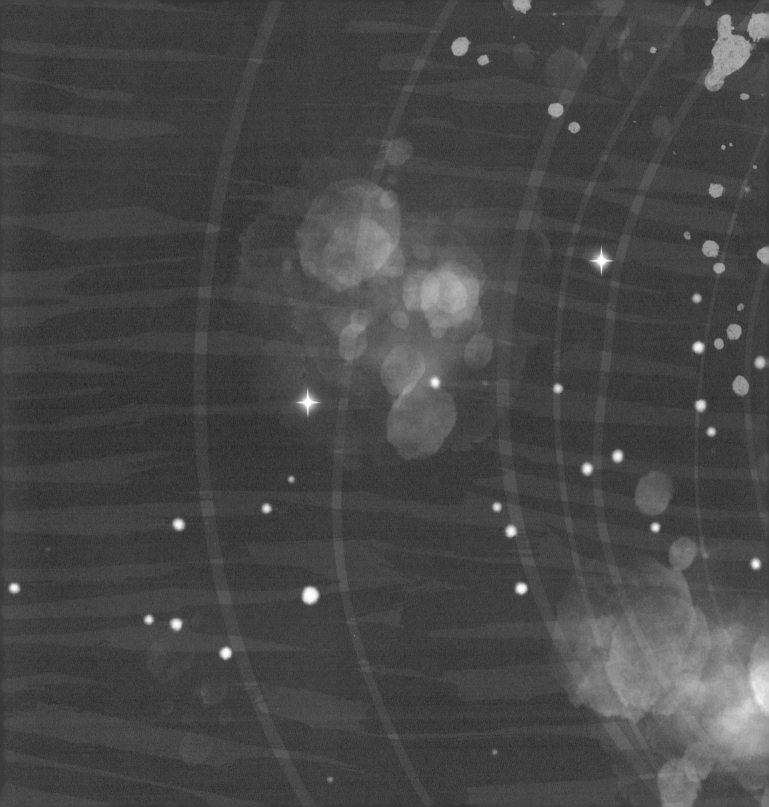

but
splash!

He missed the boat
and sunk below
into the
belly of the sea.

"Ernest! Ernest!"

Elsie cried.

"No, oh no!"

she screamed.

He couldn't swim,
Elsie knew that.
Into the depths she peered.
Moments passed.
They seemed like hours ...

The ripples disappeared.

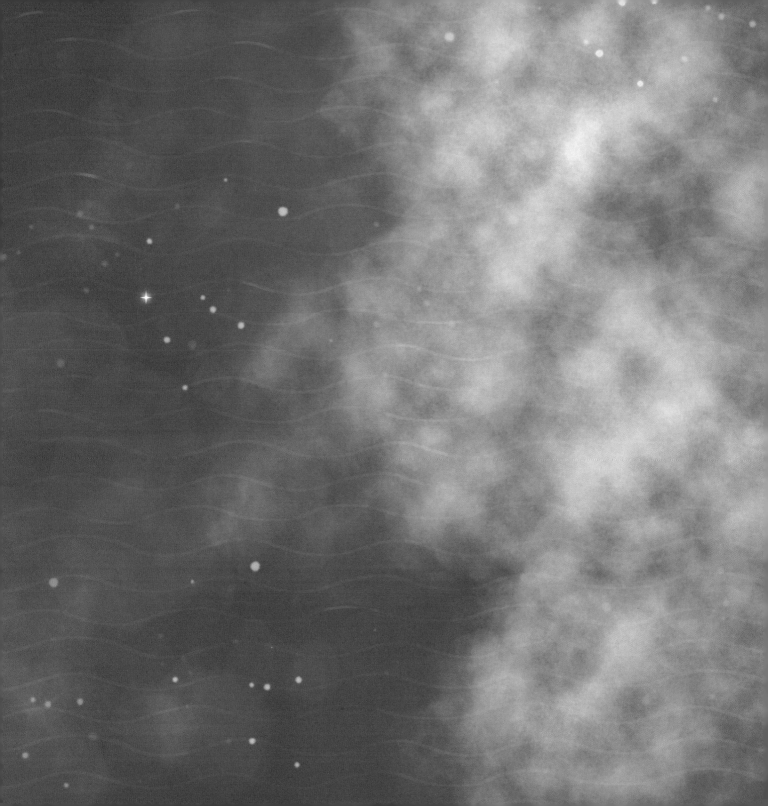

Then a bubble ...

Another there.

The surface burst again.

And up popped

a welcome sight ...

a little mouse's head.

Coughing, spluttering,

Ernest grabbed his dear wife's

outstretched paw

and with all her strength

she hauled her husband

safely back on board.

Dripping wet
and shivering cold,
Ernest said, "I'm done.
I've gone off cheese."
Elsie agreed
and they set a course
for home.

Now, no cat likes getting wet,
not even a starry one.
So he took his place amongst the stars
and left the mice alone.

An hour or two later
their boat scraped upon
that familiar, shingly beach.
They'd made it back
with their lives
if not with any cheese …

"… Or my hat," said Elsie.

"Never mind. Later on,
I'll take you shopping," Ernest said,
"and buy you another one."

"Sshhh …
Hear that?" said Elsie,
as the waves washed on the shore.
Ernest listened and he heard too
the sea softly purr …

"Little mice. Little mice.

Here's some advice …
I don't know what you've heard

but the moon is not
as you believed, quite foolishly,

made of cheese …

I'm sorry to pooh-pooh your dream.
The moon is my saucer of cream."

The mice looked up
into the sky.
Perhaps the cat
indeed was right.
The moon was round
and full and white.
A bright, milky,
creamy white.

And then they saw
the cat lap up
the moon
then turn and wink.

"Come on," said Ernest.
"Yawn ... I'm tired.
It'll be morning soon,
I think."

So arm in arm,
two little mice
left behind
the dwindling night.

And one by one
the stars went out.

The sun came up,

while in

a hole they'd made,

in the loft of a pub,

Ernest and Elsie

lay safe and snug.

Thoughts of adventure
for now would keep

as the two little mice
lay sound asleep.

The end.

Printed in Great Britain
by Amazon